THE LIGHT CHASER MYSTERIES

VANISHING LIGHTS

HORIZON BOOKS
CAMP HILL, PENNSYLVANIA

Vanishing Lights

Dedicated to
Ernest & Velma, Mike & Linda,
Bill & Bonnie, Al & Marilyn

Horizon Books
3825 Hartzdale Drive
Camp Hill, PA 17011

ISBN: 0-88965-106-X
LOC Catalog Card Number: 93-74959
Printed in the United States of America

Cover art © by Gary Watson

94 95 96 97 98   5   4   3   2   1

Book 1 of the Light Chaser Mystery Series

1

Adventure

UU

Matthew & Amie Tate
Warm Springs Ranch
Winston, New Mexico 87943

Dear Rainie,

Your uncle and I are looking forward to your visit. We have been praying that you and Ryan will have a wonderful adventure at Warm Springs Ranch.

Your mother said on the phone last week that you like puzzles and mysteries. Here's one for you. Can you figure out why our ranch brand is UU?

In answer to your questions, yes, we have

several horses and you will have plenty of
time to ride them. Please bring your swimming suits, as you'll be able to swim in the
famous warm springs called Ojo Caliente.
Apache Indians used to swim there. You'll
also be able to see the ruins of old Fort Ojo
Caliente where Geronimo was captured.
There are many other Indian ruins in the
area that I'm sure you'll enjoy exploring.

Uncle Matt will meet your flight in Albu-
querque. I'm sorry I won't be able to meet
you at the airport. We are praying for your
trip. Give our love to your mother.

Love,
Aunt Amie &
Uncle Matt

P.S. I'm excited about meeting you face to
face. Uncle Matt has said so many wonderful things about you. We are going to have
a great time together.

UU

"I feel like a dog," Ryan Trevors said without
looking up from his electronic baseball game.

Rainie ignored her brother and looked at the letter again. Her penciled margin notes read: 2 U's,
Twin U's, the horseshoes, 2 horseshoes, W, and the
double U. She was sure the last one was right. But

Rainie was worried that Ryan was going to ruin everything. She folded the letter and put it back in her bag under the seat.

"They treat us like dogs," Ryan said.

"Ignore him," Rainie said to her new friend Tracey as they looked out the plane window at the white mattresses of clouds not far below.

"They should've put us in boxes and sent us with the suitcases." Ryan held up the name tag that hung around his neck. "Then we wouldn't have to wear these. Maybe they'd like us to start barking."

Tracey couldn't stand anymore. "Does he have his shots?" she asked Rainie.

"Not distemper!" Both girls giggled.

"Just you wait," Ryan said. "I'll get you."

"Does he bite, too?" Tracey asked pulling the bill of Ryan's baseball cap over his eyes.

"Cut it out!" Ryan shouted. He adjusted his Pirates cap. "Now, I've got to start all over. And I had a good streak going, too. I'm gonna get you for this!"

Rainie wondered if they were going to get in trouble. At least Ryan hadn't hit Tracey. She glanced over her shoulder down the aisle. The stewardess hadn't noticed; she was busy picking up empty plastic cups and peanut wrappers.

"Will he really do something?" Tracey whispered.

"He'll do something; he always gets even."

"I'm sorry," Tracey said. "I didn't mean to . . ."

Rainie turned to the window. Why did her eleven-year-old little brother have to be five inches taller and twenty pounds heavier than her? Why'd she have to put up with his brattiness? She was going to be thirteen in August, old enough not to have to put up with pesty little brothers. She rubbed her black and teal bracelet between her fingers.

"That's pretty," Tracey said. "Where did you get it?"

"My Aunt Amie sent it to me for Christmas. It's braided horsehair," replied Rainie.

"Is it a friendship bracelet?"

"I guess so. She told me to pray about our visit whenever I felt it."

"What's she like?"

"I'm not sure. I've never met her. But she writes neat letters and my mom says Aunt Amie is her favorite aunt." She took off the bracelet and let Tracey try it on.

"Aren't you afraid?" Tracey asked.

"No; I met my Uncle Matt three years ago and he's really neat," answered Rainie.

"He's a preacher." Ryan said preacher like he was saying a bad word.

"He's a missionary," Rainie said. "Well, he used to be a missionary to Africa. Now he owns a ranch."

"Does he have horses?" asked Tracey.

"Yes," Rainie answered.

"And cowboys and Indians too," Ryan added.

"We'll probably get shot with a poison arrow if we do something they don't like."

"What's wrong with your brother?" Tracey asked.

"He made All Stars in baseball and because he had to come on this trip he couldn't play."

"Couldn't he have stayed home?"

"No. My mom is finishing nursing school and she is trying to study for her board exams. It would have been really hard on her if we were around. When Aunt Amie offered to have us visit, Mom thought it would be the best for us."

"Doesn't that make you mad?" asked Tracey.

"What do you mean?" Rainie responded.

"Well, being shoved out of the way."

"No, I hadn't thought of it that way. I think it's going to be an adventure."

"I'm going to see my dad and new step-mother," Tracey said. "So my mom can have some time to herself."

"Now, I see what you mean," Rainie said. "But I like my Uncle Matt because he really helped me after our dad left us."

"All he wanted to do was to get you saved," Ryan said. "I don't need to get rescued."

"Would you just play your games and keep quiet," Rainie said in a threatening tone.

"How did your uncle help you?" asked Tracey.

"He was on missionary tour," said Rainie.

"What's that?" Tracey asked.

"He was traveling to different churches in Pennsylvania telling them about his work in Africa. When Mom heard he was going to be in several churches in Pittsburgh, she made us go to church. After we heard him, he came over to our house several times."

"It was boring," Ryan said.

Rainie glared at Ryan.

"But how did he help you?" insisted Tracey.

"He told me about Jesus," Rainie answered.

"How did that help?"

"She was saved," Ryan said, as if she'd caught the worst disease in the world.

Rainie ignored him. "I asked Jesus into my life. You see after Dad left and he and Mom were divorced, it was really hard."

"I know what you mean," Tracey said.

"I really didn't know where to go. And after I asked Jesus into my life things started to change. I got involved in a youth group and Sunday school in our church."

"I still don't understand."

"Well, I worried that I might have been part of the reason for Mom and Dad's divorce. I felt guilty because sometimes I made Dad angry. I wondered if I had been a better daughter maybe Dad wouldn't have left."

"I still feel that way," Tracey said.

"Uncle Matt explained that Jesus died for me to forgive my sins. He said that no one is perfect and we all need a Savior."

"I don't need anyone to rescue me," Ryan said.

"I'm not drowning."

"Honey, would you fasten your seat belt," the stewardess said to Ryan as she passed. "We're getting ready to land."

"Dog tags and honeys. I can't stand this!" Ryan exclaimed.

Both girls laughed.

"I almost forgot." Tracey gave Rainie's bracelet back.

Rainie rolled the bracelet around and around her wrist as they landed. She prayed for Ryan and for Tracey.

After the other passengers got off, the stewardess led all the kids with "dog tags" off the plane.

She waited with them and matched their tags to the people wanting to be united with them. Tracey's dad and step-mom claimed her.

"See we're just like luggage," Ryan muttered.

Rainie looked in vain for Uncle Matt. He always wore a suit and tie. He was tall and bald on top with gray hair on the sides. He liked to tease that he was too tall for his hair and that it didn't grow above the timberline.

Other parents and grandparents came. Soon they were the only kids left.

"What does your uncle look like?" the stewardess asked.

Rainie told her. Other passengers and their friends gathered around them. Now they were being jostled as the crowd increased.

A cowboy with a tanned, leathery complexion

and gray hat pushed through the crowd toward the stewardess. He was head and shoulders taller than most of the crowd. He winked at Rainie. "I'll take these two."

"We can't go with you," Ryan said.

It was Uncle Matt's voice, but it wasn't the uncle she remembered. He looked different in his cowboy hat. He smiled at Rainie. "Uncle Matt!" she exclaimed recognizing his smile.

He unbuttoned his shirt pocket and gave the papers to the stewardess. "I guess you'll have to keep the other one," he said gesturing toward Ryan. He picked up Rainie's bag.

"Rainie, that tall, skinny thing couldn't be Ryan." Then Uncle Matt winked at Ryan and reached down and grabbed his bag.

Ryan smiled for the first time in two days.

2

Ryan's Revenge

"Wake up you two," Uncle Matt said. "We're almost there."

Rainie swept her hair out of her face and back over her shoulders. "How much farther?" she asked.

"About five miles."

Ryan looked out the truck window. "Where are the lights?"

"There's the greater light to govern the day and the lesser to govern the night," Uncle Matt said.

"What?" Ryan said in a puzzled tone.

"The sun and the moon," Rainie said.

"You mean there's no stores; no video arcades?" Ryan said in disgust. "Where will I get my baseball cards?"

"About fifty miles back," Uncle Matt said. "Why? Do you need them?"

"He collects them," Rainie said. "He has several thousand."

"Mom wouldn't let me bring them," Ryan complained. "What am I going to do out here?"

"There will be plenty of things to do," Uncle Matt said. "I hope you'll enjoy trying some new things."

"I've never seen so many stars," Rainie said, "and they look so close."

"That's because you're used to the city. The brightness of the city lights hides them."

"It's almost like I could reach out and touch them."

They approached the archway over the entrance to the ranch. It read, WARM SPRINGS RANCH and had UU on either side of the ranch name.

"What do the 2U's mean?" Ryan asked.

"Do you know Rainie?" Uncle Matt asked.

"It's the ranch brand. I think it means the Double U."

"You're right," Uncle Matt said.

A light came on as they drove between the ranch house and some corrals. Rainie could see more buildings in back. The ranch house looked like a long box with three arches on one end. A large picture window looked out on the valley toward the other end of the house. A white-haired woman looked out the window.

They unloaded their luggage and Uncle Matt showed them their rooms. "Now come meet your aunt."

The introduction caught Rainie by surprise. Aunt Amie was seated in a wheelchair.

"Matt bring the cookies and milk to the table, please. I'm sure you kids could use a little snack after your long trip."

Aunt Amie rolled over to the open end of the table. Rainie and Ryan sat down on either side of her. After Uncle Matt brought the cookies and milk, he sat at the head of the table with his back to the picture window. Then he thanked God for the food.

"Did you figure out our ranch brand?" Aunt Amie asked Rainie.

Rainie's mouth was full. She couldn't even manage a mumble.

"She sure did," Uncle Matt said.

"Thank you for putting it in your letter," Rainie said. "I enjoyed solving it."

"Your mother said you like mysteries," Aunt Amie said.

"I enjoy reading mysteries and I hope to solve some someday."

"That's great. Well, we'd better let you two get to bed," Aunt Amie said.

Uncle Matt cleared one side of the table and Rainie the other. While she picked up the last glass from the table, Uncle Matt turned out the dining room light. Something flashed in the picture window.

"What's that light?" Rainie pointed at a bright light. "Is there a house in the valley?"

Uncle Matt turned the dining room light back on. "I don't see anything. There are no lights out there and there certainly aren't any houses out that way. The closest place is the Rodriquez ranch and that's in the opposite direction."

"It went out when you turned the lights on," explained Rainie.

"Inspector Rainie rides again," Ryan teased.

Rainie knew it was coming. Ryan's payback for her tease on the plane. He told them about the dinosaur. Rainie wanted to cry every time Ryan told the story.

Once Rainie and a friend had taken a short cut across a vacant lot to her friend's house. Rainie noticed part of a bone sticking out of the ground. They dug it out and struggled together carrying it home. They were sure it was a dinosaur skull. As it turned out it was only an old draft horse skull. But how were they to know?

After Ryan finished his revenge, he went to bed satisfied and happy. Uncle Matt got a drink and then pulled the picture window draperies shut and flipped off the dining room light.

Aunt Amie tried to console Rainie, "I've got something that used to be embarrassing to me. But now I'm proud of it. I'll show you in the morning. I think you'll find we have a few things in common."

Not even the expectation of learning something special could lift Rainie's mood.

3

Mysterious Light

Rainie was exhausted, but she couldn't sleep. Ryan had made a fool of her. Now her dreams for this trip were spoiled.

She knew her mind hadn't been playing tricks. Uncle Matt had said there weren't any lights out there. She knew she'd seen a strange light, even if no one believed her. Maybe she was crazy, but then maybe . . .

Rainie threw the covers off and walked slowly from her room into the hall, letting her eyes adjust to the dark. I hope everyone's asleep, she thought as she crept with her hands outstretched, past her uncle and aunt's room, then Ryan's, and finally the bathroom.

She felt like a thief, but she had to see if the light was back. What if someone was watching the house? Maybe they were waiting for the lights to

go out. If that was the case, then the light should
be on.

She padded empty air and knew she was in the
living room. Now was the tricky part. What was
between her and the picture window? Her hands
brushed a plant. She remembered. A built-in brick
planter divided the living room from the dining
room. She was almost there. How many chairs
were around the table? Two on this side and two
on the other, then Uncle Matt's by the window and
the empty space at the other end for Aunt Amie's
wheelchair. The smooth table surface—Aunt
Amie's place; Rainie breathed a sigh of relief. So
far so good.

When she reached Uncle Matt's chair she pushed
it in and turned to find the drapery cord. The
draperies squeaked and swished as she opened
them. She looked back to the hall. Nothing moved
and no lights came on. She was safe.

She looked out the window. The light glowed,
but dimly like a fire almost burnt out. She thought
it was in the same place, but she couldn't be sure.

If she could somehow mark where it was, maybe
in the morning she could figure out where the
light had been. She hesitated to go back to her
room for a pencil or a marker, lest the light go out.
What could she use?

She reached out for the counter that divided the
kitchen and dining room, then edged her way
around the counter into the kitchen. When she
thought she was near the sink, she felt for a soap

dish. Rainie found exactly what she needed, several small soap pieces. She took one and returned to the window.

The light was still there. She stretched for her Uncle's chair and barely reached it. But what if the chair wasn't centered? She needed to remember exactly where she was standing now, so that in the morning she could be at exactly the same angle when she looked out over the valley. She felt for the corner of the table, aligned her body with the corner, took one long step, and drew a soap circle around where the light glowed through the window.

Now maybe she could sleep. Instead of edging back around the counter, she reached across the counter to drop the soap in the dish. Crash!

Uncle Matt had left his glass on the counter over the sink.

The hall light came on, while Rainie was searching for the kitchen light switch.

Uncle Matt stumbled out in his robe.

"I'm sorry, I broke a glass," apologized Rainie.

"The switch is next to the refrigerator." He walked into the bright kitchen light, blinking, then inspected the damage.

"Where's the broom and dustpan?" asked Rainie.

"In the pantry, but you'd better get some shoes on."

Rainie hurried back to her room, put her shoes on, and then returned to help. Uncle Matt already had the glass swept in a pile.

Rainie reached for the dustpan. "I'm sure sorry."

"That's okay. It's our fault; we should have left a light on." He swept the glass into the pan. "We haven't had any kids around in a long time."

"Where's the trash?" Rainie asked.

"Under the sink."

Rainie put the glass in the trash and gave the dustpan back to her uncle.

"How about a midnight snack?"suggested Uncle Matt.

Rainie was worried. Did he know? "All right," she answered.

"There's still some of the ranger cookies."

"That'd be great."

Rainie found two glasses as Uncle Matt put the container of cookies and a carton of milk on the table. Rainie gave her uncle a napkin and put one by her place. She glanced out the window as she pulled out her chair. The light was gone.

"Do you want to talk about your brother?" Uncle Matt asked. "I want to help." Rainie shrugged her shoulders and dipped a cookie in her milk. Uncle Matt did the same. "We'll have to do this more often," he said and smiled, "but without the broken glass."

"Thanks for not getting mad about the glass."

"That's okay. It was an accident."

They both ate their cookies and finished their milk.

"I can't understand. Ever since I asked Jesus into

my life, Ryan's been almost like an enemy." Rainie looked down at her glass. "The harder I try to live for the Lord the worse he gets."

"Sometimes the hardest people to love can be our own family. Remember that Jesus' brothers didn't like what He was doing at first," said Uncle Matt.

"Will Ryan ever change?" asked Rainie.

"That depends a lot on us," Uncle Matt said. "We need to love him where he's at and pray he sees his need for Jesus."

"Will you help me?"

"I'll do all I can, but the most important thing we can do is pray."

Uncle Matt prayed with Rainie. When he finished he gave Rainie's hand a squeeze and they put the plate and glasses in the sink.

As they walked down the hallway Uncle Matt said, "Don't forget, we're going to give you your first riding lesson in the morning."

Rainie wasn't excited, but she wasn't worried either. Maybe God could change Ryan's life, like He'd changed hers. When Rainie pulled the covers up she remembered the window; the draperies were still open. She rolled over. She was too exhausted to battle the dark again.

4

Morning Surprise

Rainie heaped the covers around herself and rolled over. From outside she heard a whack. She grabbed the second pillow and covered her ear and head. A dull whack still sounded at intervals. Ryan must be mad. He usually threw his baseball against the garage when he was upset.

Garage . . . she wasn't at home. The window. The riding lesson. Rainie stumbled out of bed with half the covers still wrapped around her. Her watch read 10:16. She'd probably missed her first riding lesson. She showered, dressed, and fixed her hair.

The clicking of a keyboard sounded from the other end of the house. Her aunt and uncle had an office across from the kitchen. There was no one in the living room or dining room. The office door was open a crack and the clicking came from within.

Rainie rushed to the dining room window. The soap circle was barely visible on the glass. She aligned herself with the corner of the table and looked through the circle. A brown mound that looked like it had a doorway stood on a level place just above the valley floor, called a bench. Other mounds, some bread loaf shaped were scattered in a line along the bench, but not in the soap circle. She knew it had to be some kind of ruins.

Maybe she could get Uncle Matt to take her out there later. But how could she ask him?

Rainie gazed up at the sky. She couldn't believe it was so blue and clear, like no place she'd ever seen. White clouds rose above the low hills like waves about to break. Rainie wanted to stay at the window, but the clicking called her away.

Her knock on the office door brought a cheerful, "Come in." Aunt Amie was seated in her wheelchair in front of a computer. The office walls were lined with bookshelves, except for the wall above the computer; two large maps almost covered that wall. A map of Africa and a world map had pictures of people in all the available blue spaces. Different colors of yarn connected the pictures to land. Rainie knew the pictures were prayer cards of missionaries and their families. She still had one of her aunt's and uncle's. It reminded her to pray for them.

"Excuse me," said Rainie.

"Just a second," Aunt Amie continued typing. "I need to get this down."

Aunt Amie typed with a pencil in her right hand, using it to hold down the shift key and cursor keys, while the fingers of her left hand moved all over the keyboard. Rainie was amazed.

"I'm sorry you couldn't sleep well." Aunt Amie stopped typing and turned to Rainie. "I always have problems sleeping the first few nights in a new place."

"What are you working on?" Rainie asked.

"A novel. That's what I was hinting at last night when Ryan shared your dinosaur story."

"You mean this is what you were going to show me."

"No, what I was going to show you is in the box down there." She pointed with her left hand. "Go ahead and take one out."

Rainie pulled out a new paperback book. It read, *Crisis at Bonggala*, by Amie Tate.

Rainie looked up, "This is yours?"

"No, that one's yours."

"Thank you," stuttered Rainie. She was shocked. She knew Aunt Amie had multiple sclerosis, but how could she write a book? "What kind of book is it?" she asked.

"It's the beginning of a new Christian series of adult mysteries," answered Aunt Amie.

"There are others?"

"The second one will come out this spring. I'm working on the third one now." Aunt Amie hit a few keys, waited and then turned off the computer.

"Last night you said something used to be embarrassing," said Rainie.

"It was my writing." Aunt Amie rolled her chair backward. "I'll tell you after we get you some breakfast."

They went into the kitchen.

"Are you hungry?" Aunt Amie asked.

"Not really, but I might eat a little," answered Rainie.

"How about a cinnamon roll? That should tide you over till lunch."

"That sounds great."

Aunt Amie explained where everything was and Rainie helped herself. Then Aunt Amie rolled herself down the hall. "I'll be back in a few minutes."

The distant whack of a ball against something metal could still be heard. Ryan must be really upset.

Rainie finished her breakfast and put her dishes in the sink. Then she noticed the dishwasher. It was full of clean dishes. She had almost finished putting the dishes away when Aunt Amie returned. Her face was pale—almost as white as her curly hair. Rainie thought she was in pain, but her smile tried to hide it.

"Your uncle will be happy with you. That's his job," said Aunt Amie.

Rainie hadn't thought about it, but her aunt couldn't reach most of the cupboards.

"You could help me by pulling down a few things for lunch," Aunt Amie added.

Aunt Amie directed and Rainie pulled out what

was needed.

"Why were you embarrassed about your writing?" Rainie asked.

"I worked so hard and got almost nowhere before I found out I had MS. When we were forced to retire I found out that I had been too busy to really concentrate on my writing," Aunt Amie said.

"But why would that be embarrassing?"

"My dream was like your dinosaur. I liked to talk about my dreams of being a mystery writer, but in reality they were disappointments. I was writing about things I didn't know a thing about and getting lots of rejections."

"But what changed your writing?" asked Rainie.

"When I learned I had MS, I gave my writing to the Lord," Aunt Amie answered.

"What difference did that make?"

"I stopped viewing my writing as a hobby. Instead I saw it as a ministry for the Lord. I started writing about missions, because that's what I knew the most about. I wrote about a missionary named Faith Armstrong who solves all kinds of neat mysteries in Africa. Now, it seems that God is honoring her."

Rainie helped Aunt Amie fix lunch. She didn't feel so disappointed now that she'd missed her first riding lesson, because she felt like she was learning more about herself. She loved mysteries just like Aunt Amie.

Rainie wanted to tell Aunt Amie about her

mystery, but she decided to give it to the Lord. One thing, however, puzzled Rainie. All the time they were fixing lunch and Aunt Amie was explaining her novels, Ryan's baseball whack kept echoing from the yard. What happened to Ryan at the first riding lesson?

5

Crow Hopped

Ryan was still throwing his baseball at a five gallon metal bucket at lunchtime. Uncle Matt told his two cowhands, "I think it's best to leave Ryan alone right now."

"Rainie, this is Antonio Valdez," Uncle Matt said. "We call him, Val. Val, this is my niece Rainie. When they're working, the cowhands join us for meals."

Val took off his hat and bowed his head. "It's good to meet you, Miss Rainie." His black hair was streaked with gray on the sides and Rainie had never seen anyone smile as big and bright. She shook his outstretched hand.

The other cowboy was looking at the floor. He didn't appear to be any taller than Ryan and his legs bowed like a wishbone. His mustache looked like a gray waterfall that overflowed his mouth. It was going to be an event just watching him eat.

"Rainie, this is Cinch," said Uncle Matt.

Cinch took off his hat and reached out his hand.

Cinch, like Uncle Matt, was bald with a gray fringe. Rainie knew there was a story behind his name and took mental note to try and find out. She shook his hand, but he barely looked up.

The three men took off their hats and laid them on the planter.

"Val, would you say grace?" Uncle Matt asked.

"Father," Val prayed, "help this boy not to be mad at us. We know that he needs you. Forgive us for hurting his feelings. Thank you for this food that you have provided for us. Amen."

Rainie wondered what had happened to Ryan. As they ate, the story of the first riding lesson came out. And it was almost as bad as Rainie's dinosaur disaster.

While Uncle Matt did some chores, Val and Cinch had given Ryan his first lesson. But Ryan didn't want to ride the old white horse they had saddled.

"Why can't I ride that gray one with black legs?" Ryan asked.

"That's what we call a grulla," Val said. "But that's Cinch's horse, Crow Hop."

"Can't I ride him?" insisted Ryan.

"Boy, have you ever ridden anything besides those plastic horses in front of grocery stores?" Cinch asked.

"I rode a pony once in the park," Ryan said. "I'm

sure I can ride him."

"But you haven't ever been on a horse like Crow Hop," Val said. "Let us lead you around on Blanco for a while, then you can try on your own."

"Let him ride him," Cinch said. "It'd be good for him."

"But Mr. Tate might not be pleased," Val said.

"Aw . . . we'll make sure he doesn't get hurt."

Cinch took the saddle off Blanco and saddled Crow Hop. He held the reins while Val helped Ryan up.

Ryan sat in the saddle and said, "See!"

Crow Hop jumped up and down in place. Cinch still held the reins. In less than ten seconds Ryan was airborne and landed in a heap in Val's arms.

"See what?" Cinch asked. "Now you know why he's called Crow Hop. He likes to show his independence in the morning."

Ryan ran from the corral and then started punishing the bucket on the hill behind the house.

When Val had finished the story, they noticed how loud the last whack had sounded.

"That boy's had a hard time," Aunt Amie said. Her stern look caused Val and Cinch to look down at their plates.

"He'll be all right," Uncle Matt said. "I'll talk to him after lunch."

"I tried to introduce him to Ready," Val said, "but he wouldn't have anything to do with us."

"That boy sure is stubborn," Cinch said.

Aunt Amie's hard, brown-eyed glance quieted

Cinch. He looked down at his plate again.

"Who's Ready?" Rainie asked.

"Ready's our blue heeler. He's a cattle dog," Aunt Amie said.

"Uncle Matt could you take me out to see those ruins that Aunt Amie wrote me about?" Rainie asked.

"Sure," Uncle Matt said, "but you'll have to put the dishes in the dishwasher. I've got to talk with your brother."

"Boy, this is just like home . . . work before you play," exclaimed Rainie. She spent the rest of lunch trying not to be conspicuous about watching Cinch eat. He'd part his waterfall mustache in the middle, put in a mouthful or two, then part it again. It was amazing.

After the men left, Rainie was putting the dirty dishes in the dishwasher when she asked Aunt Amie, "Why is Cinch called Cinch?"

"The part of a saddle that holds the saddle on the horse is a cinch," Aunt Amie explained. "With people Cinch is tight as a cinch. He just doesn't know how to get along very well with people, but with animals it's different. He's the best in the area at doctoring horses, cows, and dogs."

"Does Val know the Lord?" Rainie asked.

"Yes, but he's a new Christian."

"He seemed pretty upset about what happened to Ryan."

"Val forgets sometimes and lets Cinch lead him along," Aunt Amie said. "But you'll seldom meet a nicer person. I'm sure he'll give you a riding lesson tomorrow."

"Not on Crow Hop," Rainie said and then smiled.

"On Blanco," Aunt Amie snapped. They both laughed. Then they noticed the whacking had stopped.

6

Diamond Tracks

Uncle Matt threw a towel to Rainie and one to Ryan as they climbed in the pickup.

"Where are we going to swim?" Ryan asked.

"At the spring called Ojo Caliente," said Uncle Matt.

"It means Warm Springs," Rainie said. "That's where the ranch got its name."

They had barely driven out the ranch gate when they came to a barbed-wire gate. Uncle Matt stopped, opened the gate, then drove through. "Do you think you can close it, Ryan?"

Ryan hesitated, then said, "I can try."

Uncle Matt watched in the side mirror as Ryan struggled with the gate. He yelled back at Ryan, "Pull up the bottom wire loop first, then put the top one on."

Ryan pulled up the bottom loop, and the top fit

over easily.

"Good job," Uncle Matt said. "You learn fast."

Rainie noticed the view for the first time. In the midday light the rock formation in front of them was green and gray. From a distance one might have mistaken it for a solid rock wall, but a slash like a thin V, cut from the top to the bottom. A creek ran through the narrow gap. And the two track road they were on met at the gap.

"It looks like the road and the creek meet down there," Rainie said as she pointed.

"That's the Monticello Box," Uncle Matt said. "The creek bed is the road. Some places it is barely wide enough for a pickup to get through."

"You drive down that!" Ryan exclaimed.

"Lots of times," Uncle Matt said. "We'll probably drive down it sometime while you're here."

"But isn't a box canyon a dead end?" Rainie asked.

"Not around here," Uncle Matt explained. "It's a high-walled canyon."

"Is this part of your ranch?" Rainie asked.

"No, the spring rights are owned by the community of Monticello and the ruins are on part of the Rodriquez place. I've got permission for us to be here though."

"What do you mean?" Ryan asked.

"I asked Mr. Rodriquez if we could visit the ruins today. Lots of people don't even bother to ask. They think because the ruins and springs are here, they can visit them any time they want."

"Why don't they ask?" Rainie asked.

"Well, because many think it's government land. Or others, because it's a famous place, they feel they have a right to visit it."

Uncle Matt stopped and turned off the truck. They were right across the creek from the ruins Rainie wanted to see.

"But why is it famous?" Ryan asked.

"This was the reservation for the Warm Springs Apaches; over 1,200 Apaches lived here at one time. That's why the fort was here. This was also the only place where Geronimo was ever captured."

"Why isn't it a park?" Rainie asked.

"I suppose because it's so far off the beaten track. But it may not be private land much longer."

"What?" Rainie looked puzzled.

"There's a move to make it a national monument and preserve the ruins."

"What's wrong with that?" Ryan asked.

"There're rumors that the government could take our land."

"Could they really do that?" Rainie asked. "Could they take your ranch?"

"They wouldn't take it. They'd probably buy it, but many ranchers are afraid the park might be larger than just a preserve for the ruins. If that's the case, then many ranchers could lose land they can't afford to lose."

"What do you mean can't afford to lose?" asked Ryan.

"It takes a lot of land to run cattle around here. And some ranchers would go out of business, because they wouldn't have enough land for their cattle."

"What are you going to do?" asked Rainie.

"I'm going to let the Lord take care of it, because I know He'll take good care of me." Uncle Matt opened his door. "Are you two going to ask questions all day?"

Uncle Matt led them to the creek. Numerous smaller creeks spread out like fingers across the valley. Shades of green from dark to light stretched from the creeks to the valley sides, as though a giant leaf was painted on the valley floor. The finger creeks were the veins of the leaf and the shades of green its lobes.

They jumped rock to rock and zigzagged back and forth across the creeks until they came to tall grass on the other side.

"I think the spring must have been above ground when the soldiers were here," Uncle Matt explained. "It's underground now. That's why this grass is so lush."

"Is that why it's so green over there near the pickup?" Rainie asked as she pointed at a small stand of cottonwood trees surrounded by a carpet of green.

"Yes, there are springs underground all over the valley."

Uncle Matt led them across the grassy meadow and up a small hill to the bench top. The ruins were a low line of broken mounds.

"They look like termite hills in Africa," Rainie said.

"How would you know that?" Uncle Matt asked. "That's what I thought the first time I saw them."

"Educational TV," Rainie said.

Uncle Matt laughed as they walked side by side to the fort. Grasshoppers skipped through the grass ahead of them with an irritated clicking sound, as though they were saying, "Don't disturb us." Then Ryan almost jumped out of his skin when he flushed a cottontail rabbit from a bush.

The outlines of individual adobe bricks were visible now. "This wasn't a walled fort; the buildings themselves served as protection," Uncle Matt explained.

"How old is this?" Ryan asked.

"Oh, about a hundred and fifteen years or so. It was built between 1874 and 1877, and then abandoned in 1882."

"Where did you learn about the fort?" Rainie asked.

"When my brother Mitch died and left me the ranch, I was going through some of his papers. I found a file crammed full of articles, clippings, and studies on Ojo Caliente. I read them and have since added to them."

Uncle Matt continued to explain as he showed Rainie and Ryan the outline of the fort. Rainie thought Ryan would be bored, but he didn't complain a bit.

"What's that big hole?" Rainie asked, leaning over a low wall and pointing at the hole. It looked like a well; a large limb stuck up from the bottom.

"That's never been there before that I remember," commented Uncle Matt.

Rainie was sure this was the part of the fort where she'd seen the light. The reflection of the picture window of her uncle's home shone across the valley in the afternoon sun. "What's the limb for?" Rainie asked.

Uncle Matt looked over the wall. Someone's probably used it to climb in and out of that hole."

"Do you think it's been dug recently?" asked Rainie.

"It's been here since the last rain. Most of the dirt's crusted over," answered Uncle Matt.

Rainie ducked her head and walked through the doorway.

After only a moment, she called out, "Look what I found! Someone's tracks!" Rainie knelt down by some loose dirt in the corner opposite the hole.

Uncle Matt entered the building and knelt next to Rainie. "Those are fresh," he said.

A diamond shape was pressed in the insole of a boot track about two inches from the front of the heel. "This has to be . . ." Rainie stopped.

"What?" Uncle Matt said with a puzzled look.

7

Geronimo and Buffalo Soldiers

"What kind of boot made this?" Rainie asked.

"Some kind of western boot." Uncle Matt stood up. "Remind me to get you a hat when we get back to the truck."

Ryan was sitting in the shade of a wall surveying the valley. Rainie and Uncle Matt sat down next to him.

"Why does the fort look this way?" Ryan asked.

"I'm sure people took the lumber from the roofs and some of the adobe bricks to build other buildings, but the weather also helped. The rain melted the adobe down to these dirt mounds." Uncle Matt waved his arm in the direction of a row of mounds. "Treasure hunters and artifact collectors did a lot of the damage too."

"What about the hole?" Rainie asked.

"Maybe bottle hunters, but I don't think the soldiers had a latrine inside a building."

Both Rainie and Ryan gave their uncle puzzled looks.

"Sometimes bottle hunters find the plans of forts or towns. They figure out where the outhouses were and then dig for them," explained Uncle Matt.

"Why?" Ryan asked.

"Because the soldiers dropped their bottles down them."

"Gross," Rainie exclaimed.

"Don't be silly," Ryan said. "It's dirt by now."

Uncle Matt pulled his hat over his eyes and chuckled. "I wish you two could stay longer. I haven't had this much fun in years."

"Is this where Geronimo was captured?" Rainie asked.

As they rested in the shade, Uncle Matt told them how twenty-four-year-old John Clum, an Indian agent from the Apache Reservation at San Carlos, Arizona had been ordered to capture Geronimo. John Clum had only a hundred Apache policemen with him when he came to capture Geronimo, whereas thousands of soldiers had already failed.

Uncle Matt pointed across the valley. "Clum knew that Geronimo and his men were in the hills. He left eighty of his men in the hills behind us and rode into the fort with twenty."

"How many men did Geronimo have?" asked Ryan.

"One hundred," Uncle Matt said. "Clum sent word to Geronimo that he wanted to talk to him about surrender in the morning. During the night the rest of Clum's men sneaked in and hid in the buildings." Uncle Matt used his thumb like a hitchhiker to indicate the ruins behind them.

"When Geronimo saw only twenty men with Clum, he thought he was going to take some easy scalps. He came down from the hills with all of his men. Clum asked him to surrender. When Geronimo wouldn't, Clum's hidden men stuck their rifles through the windows, all pointed at Geronimo."

Uncle Matt stopped and smiled, "I'm getting thirsty."

"What happened?" Ryan asked.

"Geronimo surrendered and was captured for the first and only time."

"What else happened here?" Rainie asked. Ryan leaned forward elbows on his knees; he only did that when he was watching a good baseball game.

"Lew Wallace, the territorial governor of New Mexico visited here once," said Uncle Matt.

"What's so great about him?" Ryan asked.

"He wrote the book *Ben Hur*," Uncle Matt answered.

"That's one of Mom's favorite movies," Rainie said.

"I know," said Ryan.

"I was telling Uncle Matt!" Rainie exclaimed.

"Also, the famous Apache chiefs Mangas Coloradas and Cochise stayed here on and off." Uncle Matt then pointed to the large mountain across the canyon, above the cedar and juniper spotted hills. Its face and top were blue-green with pine trees. "That's Vick's Peak. It's named for Victorio, another Apache Chief."

"What'd he do?" Ryan asked.

"Victorio and his braves raided the fort, captured forty-six horses and killed eight Buffalo Soldiers."

"Where'd they keep the buffalo?" Ryan asked.

Uncle Matt turned red with laughter.

Ryan turned to Rainie and lifted his open palms as though to ask, "What'd I say?"

Uncle Matt stood up. "I'm sorry," he smiled and said, "I should've explained earlier." He told Ryan and Rainie about the Buffalo Soldiers as they followed him back to the truck.

"After the Civil War many of the freed slaves joined the military. When Indians saw these black soldiers, they called them Buffalo Soldiers because their black curly hair reminded them of the curly hair of buffalo."

"So you're telling me there weren't any buffalo," Ryan said as he laughed.

"Not then. Most of the big herds had moved north and the ones in the south had been wiped out."

Uncle Matt opened the passenger side door and

reached behind the seat. "Here," he handed Rainie a blue cap that said SIERRA FEED AND WESTERN WEAR. "That's where your Aunt got your bracelet. You might as well have a cap to go with it."

"Thanks," Rainie said as she adjusted the cap on her head.

"I'm just protecting myself," Uncle Matt said. "I don't know what your aunt would do if I let you get cooked."

He looked at Rainie's freckled nose and cheeks. "You're not well done. I'd say medium. You'll have to wear it while you're swimming."

Ryan laughed.

Uncle Matt pulled Ryan's cap over his eyes. "You'll have to wear yours, too."

Rainie was worried. What was Ryan going to do?

Ryan straightened his cap and grinned.

8

Waters Stirred

After a cool drink, they followed the path and drove through a spring that flowed around the base of another bench.

"There's a large pueblo ruin above the head of this spring," Uncle Matt said. "I'll take you there another day."

The track turned and ran up and along the bench toward Monticello Box. The massive jagged walls stood almost before them. A rock spine like a dragon's back rose on the canyon's right side and a hill shaped like the large knuckle on a person's fist rose on the left.

Uncle Matt stopped below the knuckle shaped hill where a side canyon joined the main one. Water rushed from the canyon and joined the spring they'd just crossed. The lazy creek that flowed with its many fingers through the valley floor on the fort's side was separated from the other side of the canyon by a sand bar. All the water met at the narrow gash of the box.

"I hope you brought your swimming suits," said Uncle Matt.

"We've got them on underneath," Ryan said.

"I can't believe all this water. There was none by the ranch," Rainie said.

"Most of it flows out of the ground this side of the Double U," explained Uncle Matt.

"Can we walk down the box?" Rainie asked.

"After you've gone swimming I'll take you part way down."

"Where are we going swimming?" Ryan asked.

"The pool is about two hundred yards up the canyon. When you start seeing the top of a cotton-wood tree, you'll know we're almost there."

"Is this the trail?" Ryan asked.

It only took a nod from Uncle Matt, and Ryan was gone.

"Will he be all right?" Rainie asked.

"He'll be fine."

The trail crisscrossed the creek a dozen times before they saw the cottonwood. They jumped or balanced on rocks to ford it. In places the canyon floor looked like a waterslide where the water had cut through the rock. Small waterfalls cascaded white in other places.

Dark green grass as stiff and thick as a paintbrush lined the creek. Wildflowers in purples, reds, yellows and whites poked through and above the grass. Orange butterflies flitted flower to flower. Loud chirps of crickets blended with the rush and ripples of the water.

"A snake!" Ryan called from ahead.

"Great," Rainie said.

"It's probably just a garter snake," said Uncle Matt as he strode to take the lead.

"It got away," Ryan reported. "This pool doesn't look very deep."

Rainie had never seen anything so clear. The pool was about the size of a motel swimming pool. But it shimmered in a strange way.

"It's about two and a half feet deep," Uncle Matt said.

"Look at the fish!" Ryan shouted. A school of three to four inch fish swam back and forth.

"They look like they're encased in plastic," Rainie said.

"Wow," Ryan said, "like those bugs in plastic bubbles in the airport gift shop."

"Why does it shimmer so much?" Rainie asked.

"Because of all the water coming up." Uncle Matt pointed at a flat rock, "Put your towels there and I'll show you something." They walked back behind the screen of trees at the head of the pool.

"Where's the spring?" Ryan asked.

"It's flowing up from the bottom of the pool," Uncle Matt said. "Why don't you go for a swim?"

Ryan and Rainie stripped down to their swimming suits and waded into the water. Uncle Matt threw them their hats.

"It's warm," Ryan said.

"And nice," said Rainie.

Uncle Matt rolled up his pants and took off his boots. "These old legs haven't seen the light of day in years."

"A ghost," Ryan teased and glided to the other end of the pool. Rainie retrieved his hat.

When she looked back Uncle Matt was seated on the rock dam, dangling his white feet and legs in the water. Several orange dragonflies hovered like helicopters over the pool.

"Come back to this end and sit up here with me," he called.

They splashed each other as they made their way back to Uncle Matt. While they were getting settled on either side of him, he said, "Watch the water."

The water they'd stirred up cleared in less than fifteen seconds.

They went out and thrashed in the water again, just to see it clear.

"Sin is like that kids," Uncle Matt said. "It stirs up our lives and Christ is the only one who can make it calm again."

"Is that why you brought us up here?" Ryan asked.

"Partly," said Uncle Matt, "and this is the place where the Apaches came if they were sick or injured."

"You mean Geronimo and Victorio swam here." Ryan's eyes were wide with astonishment.

"Yes," Uncle Matt said, "this spring and the land around here is part of the reason they fought."

"Wow, Matt, give me some sunglasses," a deep voice sounded from behind them; "your legs are blinding me."

Rainie turned around to see two men standing by the edge of the water.

"Hi Jim. This is my niece Rainie and my nephew Ryan."

The shorter of the two men tipped his hat.

"This is Jim Holton and Will Yancey. They ranch down below the box."

The taller didn't even acknowledge the greeting.

"We saw your truck below and decided to come up," Jim said.

"We got tired of waiting," Yancey said. "We came to tell you there's a meeting at the Monticello Fire Station tomorrow night at 6:00."

"What's it about?" asked Uncle Matt.

"About the government taking our land," Yancey said louder than necessary. "I'll see you there." He turned and started back down the trail.

"What's going on, Jim?" Uncle Matt asked.

"Yancey called this meeting so we can unite against those who want to take our land." Jim kicked the ground as he spoke. It seemed like he didn't want to look Uncle Matt in the eye. "I hope you can be there."

"I'll try," Uncle Matt responded.

"It'll mean a lot to Yancey. I'd better catch up." He disappeared down the trail.

"You two better get your clothes on," Uncle Matt said as he rubbed his chin.

They watched as the waters cleared after they got out.

"It sounds to me like somebody's been stirring the waters around here," Uncle Matt said, "and it might take a miracle from our Lord to calm them."

9

Night Riders

"There are two ways back," Uncle Matt said; "a high way and a low one. The high one's faster and there's an Indian ruin toward the end."

"I'd like to follow the creek back," Rainie said. As she'd dried off and dressed, she looked at the ground where Jim Holton had scuffed it, but there wasn't a diamond shape in his track. If she followed the creek, maybe she could find Will Yancey's tracks.

"We'll come back here again, won't we?" Ryan asked.

"Sure," said Uncle Matt.

"If you take the high trail, can I take the one along the creek?" asked Rainie.

"That'll be fine," Uncle Matt said. "We'll be able to see you from above."

As they turned to go Uncle Matt said, "Watch for the two-step snakes."

"What?" Rainie said.

"If they bite you, just stand still."

"Right," Rainie said; "two steps and you're dead."

Ryan and Uncle Matt laughed.

Rainie guessed it was a man's joke. She wondered sometimes about her uncle's sense of humor. But then she admired him for his almost continuous cheerful spirit. In spite of his brother's death, Aunt Amie's sickness, their forced retirement from the mission field, and the adjustment to a new occupation, his joyfulness flowed out. She knew it had to be from the Lord because she could already see its affect on Ryan. As she walked, Rainie kept her eyes on the ground.

"What took you so long?" asked Ryan as he looked up to see Rainie join them. He had his shoes off and pants rolled up. "We're going to wade down to the box."

"I was listening to the sounds of the water." Which was true, but she had also been looking for clear tracks. She didn't want to tell Ryan what she had been doing. "I couldn't hear the water before," Rainie teased, "because someone was chattering so much."

"I'd say she didn't get wet enough before," Uncle Matt said. He grabbed her and acted like he was going to throw her in.

"No, Uncle Matt," yelled Rainie.

"Then quit complaining and get your shoes off."

Ryan and Rainie waded ankle to knee deep toward the box. Uncle Matt walked next to them on the sand bar. As Ryan and Rainie stepped around a boulder, a school of fish rushed to get away and ran into their feet.

"Piranha," Uncle Matt yelled.

Both kids jumped to the sand at his feet.

Uncle Matt almost fell backward with laughter. Ryan and Rainie jumped back into the stream and splashed him, until he fled from its edge. He walked across the sand bar and waited for them at the entrance to the box.

"It tickles," Ryan said, as schools of frightened fish were pushed into their feet by the current.

"I've never felt anything like it before," Rainie replied.

"How far can we go?" Ryan asked when they reached Uncle Matt.

"Not too far. We're going to drive through it tomorrow."

"Can we go with you to the meeting?" Rainie asked.

"If you want to," answered Uncle Matt.

The water flowed a foot deep through the box. Walls several hundred feet high rose above them. Cactus and brush grew in the cracks and on the ledges. Cliff swallows darted in and out of their circular mud nests.

Rainie and Ryan still waded; Uncle Matt climbed on rocks along the edge.

"Are these horse tracks?" Rainie pointed in the

mud where the box widened out a little.

"Yes," said Uncle Matt. "I noticed some back at the entrance, too."

"But I thought those ranchers drove through in a pickup," said Rainie.

"They did. Look here." Uncle Matt pointed where tire tracks had rolled over the horse tracks.

"Then who came through on horses and when?" Rainie asked as she glanced up the canyon. "We would have seen them."

"Inspector Rainie rides again," taunted Ryan.

Rainie chased Ryan back splashing him all the way.

"We'd better get back. Your aunt's going to have supper waiting for us," Uncle Matt called.

At supper, Uncle Matt and Ryan retold the day's events for Val, Cinch, and Aunt Amie's benefit, including the Buffalo Soldiers and the piranha. The only thing that sobered the otherwise enjoyable time was Uncle's Matt's announcement of the meeting in Monticello. Cinch and Val agreed. Someone was stirring up trouble.

While Rainie put the dishes in the dishwasher she took mental account of the clues. She felt sure someone with a diamond shape on his boot was riding up the box at night to do something that he couldn't do by day. Maybe learning more about the box would answer some questions. Couldn't someone simply drive up the box to the ruins? Why ride a horse?

When Rainie finished, she slipped a piece of soap in her pocket. Uncle Matt and Ryan were watching a baseball game on TV, and Aunt Amie was writing in her office. The office door was slightly ajar.

Rainie stuck her head around the door, "Excuse me."

"Come in," Aunt Amie responded as she continued typing. "Just a minute."

Rainie waited until she finished. Then she asked, "How's your mystery coming?"

"Fine. How's yours?" Aunt Amie smiled.

"I'm sorry," Rainie said, "I should have told you about the soap."

"I don't know what you're talking about," Aunt Amie said. "I meant the mysterious tracks. Your uncle told me about them."

"You mean the tracks at the fort?"

"And in the box," Aunt Amie added. "He thinks you might be on to something."

Rainie didn't know what to say. She didn't know if she was quite ready to risk another possible "dinosaur" embarrassment if all her ideas turned out to be nothing.

"Did you find any tracks by the spring?" persisted her aunt.

Rainie laughed, "You're better at this than I am."

"I've had a little practice," Aunt Amie said. "How can I help you?"

"I didn't find any tracks by the spring," Rainie said, "but I was curious about Jim Holton and Will Yancey."

"Jim Holton has ranched here all his life. He tries to do as much as he can to help the youth in the community. I think he does all right at ranching. At least he doesn't have to hold down a day job like some of the smaller ranchers."

"Have you heard anything bad about him?"

"Only that his son is a real trouble maker."

"What about Will Yancey?" asked Rainie.

"He hasn't ranched here very long. About a year longer than us. Your uncle said he was pretty rude today," answered Aunt Amie.

"Yeah," Rainie said, "kind of bossy, I'd say."

"What is this about the soap?"

"I borrowed a little piece from the kitchen. I'll tell you about it tomorrow."

"Speaking of tomorrow," said Aunt Amie as she glanced at her watch, "you'd better get to bed."

After everyone had gone to bed, Rainie sneaked back to the picture window. The light was there. The same dim glow, but it looked further up the bench from the fort ruins. Rainie circled it on the glass. The light glowed then vanished. She'd check it out in the morning. Maybe her aunt and uncle were right; maybe she really was on to something.

10

Precious Pottery

While Rainie cleared the breakfast dishes, Uncle Matt had a second cup of coffee. "Is there another ruin close to the fort?" Rainie asked. She was worried that he'd noticed the soap circles when he stood and looked out the window.

"There's one on the point of the bench, next to where the arroyo runs into the valley."

"What's an arroyo?" Rainie wondered.

"Oh, it's a deep gully that sometimes carries a stream," Uncle Matt answered.

Rainie pointed, "Is it there at that bunch of junipers?"

"How you'd know?" asked Uncle Matt.

"I'll tell you tonight, if you take me over there today."

Uncle Matt raised his eyebrows. "More detective work?"

"I'll tell you tonight."

"It's a deal," Uncle Matt said, "but you'd better hurry outside or you'll miss your riding lesson."

Ryan didn't complain once about riding Blanco. Rainie rode a brown mare with a white face named Sis. Ryan led and Rainie followed as they rode in circles around the corral. Val and Cinch sat on the top fence rail watching.

"They'll do," Val said.

"I guess so," said Cinch, "but we'll have to get that boy a real hat."

Uncle Matt came out of the house and stood with his arms resting on the top rail. "They'll be ready for the trail in a few days," he said. Rainie and Ryan smiled.

"Go ahead and dismount, get a drink and then come back to the truck," Uncle Matt said. "We've got to satisfy a young woman's curiosity."

Ryan had no problem with the gate, either opening or closing. When he climbed back in the truck Uncle Matt said, "You'll make a hand yet." Ryan beamed.

They parked across the creek from the bench's point. Rainie couldn't see any evidence of a ruin. Even after they forded the creek she couldn't see the ruin. The bench was much lower at the point than at the fort. There was almost no climb.

"This is a cobble pueblo," Uncle Matt said. "The Mimbres Indians used cobble stones and mud from the creek bed to build their walls."

Mounds of cobbles and some flat stones had been used to form a large circle. The mounds stood about three or four feet above the rest of the bench level. Within the mounds smaller circles, like cells two and three abreast, ran around the larger circle. The area in the middle was flat.

"The small stone circles are individual rooms. There might have been fifty rooms in this village. The center must have been a plaza," Uncle Matt explained. He paused and then pointed at his feet.

"Wow," Ryan said as he looked at a white piece of pottery with a black curved design on it. Rainie picked up the pottery shard.

"The Mimbres Indians made that too," Uncle Matt said. "They lived here from about 1,000 to 1,500 A.D. Did you notice anything unusual about that piece?"

"It's painted on the inside," Rainie said.

"Right. The Mimbres potter was more concerned with the inside of the pot than the outside. That's the way God is with us. He's more concerned with what we are on the inside; that's why he sent Jesus to die for us."

"Uncle Matt." Ryan pointed at a lizard sunning itself on a rock. It looked like it was doing pushups, pushing up and down from the rock. "What is it?"

"A whip-tailed lizard. I think it knows you want to catch it."

Ryan missed as he jumped with cupped hands.

Rainie turned toward the other side of the ruin

and noticed what looked like fresh turned soil. "Uncle Matt come look at this." Rainie pointed at a track with a diamond in it.

"You knew it was going to be here," Uncle Matt said, "didn't you?"

Rainie nodded; she felt like she'd found a treasure. "Why were they digging here?"

"They're looking for pots and bowls," Uncle Matt said. "Mimbres' pottery is worth thousands of dollars. In fact, not long ago I heard that a Mimbres bowl sold for almost $40,000."

"Can we dig too?" pleaded Ryan.

"No," Uncle Matt said. "The Mimbres people made much of their pottery as burial offerings and buried them with their dead. It's against the law to dig in graves."

"I thought these round rooms were their homes," Rainie exclaimed.

"When someone died they sealed the body in a room," explained Uncle Matt.

"So there could be hundreds of thousands of dollars worth of pottery in this ruin?" Rainie asked.

"Maybe, but most of it is probably long gone."

"It looks like they disturbed three rooms last night," said Rainie.

"Your diamond track is a pot hunter," Uncle Matt said. "I guess your mystery is over."

Rainie wasn't so sure. She had a feeling that the mystery had just begun. After closer examination, Rainie noticed that the rooms weren't together. Why would they dig so far apart on this side of the

ruin? She looked at her uncle's ranch house; only
one of the rooms was visible from the picture window. The others were screened from the ranch
view by juniper trees.

"Come over here," Uncle Matt called from some
juniper trees behind the ruin.

Rainie saw that he had knelt down on the
ground. As she started toward him, she caught
sight of something black and shiny out of the
corner of her eye. A small piece of black plastic
stuck out from under a flat rock. It was the corner
of what looked like a garbage bag, but the plastic
seemed heavier.

Rainie put the plastic corner in her pocket and
walked to where her uncle was kneeling.

"The horses were tied here," Uncle Matt said.
"Here's diamond tracks again."

"What are we going to do?" Rainie asked.

"I'm not sure we can do anything unless we can
figure out who's doing this."

Rainie thought that they could hide by the ruins
and then catch the pot hunters, but then she
remembered the fort. They hadn't been at the same
place twice. Where would they strike next? And
why would pot hunters be at the fort?

"Uncle Matt, can I borrow your file on Ojo
Caliente?" asked Rainie.

"Sure," he said, "if you think it will help. We'd
better get back for lunch."

"Wait," Rainie said as she pulled the plastic out
of her pocket and handed it to her uncle. "I found

it sticking out from under a rock where the pot hunters had been digging."

"Umm," Uncle Matt examined it. "It might be the corner of a tarp."

"What?"

"A piece of plastic you put down when you're painting," answered Uncle Matt.

"Could it be used for a tent?" asked Rainie.

"Sure it would keep out rain, but what would it be doing out here?"

Rainie just smiled. She knew, but she didn't want to share her secrets yet. Maybe this evening after she'd looked at the file and gone to the meeting. She felt sure the meeting would reveal something.

11

Downed Again

Rainie wished she was with the kids playing in the Monticello town square. The meeting confused her. She couldn't tell rumor from fact, or who was for who. All she knew was that there were a lot of angry people, especially Will Yancey. And there was no way to search for a diamond shape on somebody's boot without being noticed.

Ryan had said the meeting would be boring. He was playing catch with Carl McDaniel. The McDaniel place was the last one before you entered the box. The road up the creek bed ran right past their place. If anyone went by at night, the McDaniels would know. Rainie made a mental note to add that to her list.

That afternoon she'd made a list of suspects and clues, but it hadn't helped her much yet. And the

Ojo Caliente file hadn't revealed anything. One thing she'd decided was that there was more than just pot hunting involved. Why was "diamond track" at the fort the first night?

She'd been a little disappointed when they drove down the box earlier. It was so late in the day that most of the box was clothed in shadows. But one thing stuck in her mind from the drive. There was an Indian petroglyph about two miles above the McDaniels'. The Mimbres Indians had etched out a picture high on the walls above the creek bed. They'd carved hand and foot holds in the stone face so they could make the pyramid design. It looked like one of those Aztec step-pyramids that she'd seen in books and on TV, but it only had five steps on each side.

"Some folks think it points to a ruin around here," Uncle Matt had said. "Others think it might be like the road signs we use today." For some reason the words "like a road sign" were stuck in Rainie's mind.

Uncle Matt hadn't said anything the whole meeting. He just sat and listened.

Jim Holton tried to get Will Yancey elected chairman of a group to fight the establishment of a national monument. "We need someone to represent us," Jim said as he pointed to Will Yancey. "Someone who will go to Santa Fe and make the governor listen."

The group agreed that someone needed to represent them, but they couldn't agree on who.

A girl with long black hair yawned and then slipped out of the meeting. Rainie looked over her shoulder.

"Why don't you go join the other kids?" whispered Uncle Matt.

Rainie slipped out and ran to catch up with the girl who was walking toward the square. "Wait up," she hollered.

The girl turned and stopped.

"I'm Rainie Trevors; my uncle is Matt Tate."

"I'm Mary Yancey."

They turned the corner and walked toward the town square.

"What grade are you going into?" Rainie asked.

"I'm going to be a sophomore. How about you?"

"I'm going into seventh."

Ryan was still playing catch with Carl McDaniel.

"Is that your brother?" Mary asked.

"Yes, that's Ryan. How'd you know?" asked Rainie.

"My dad said the preacher had a niece and nephew staying with him." Mary emphasized preacher the same way Ryan did.

They sat down on a picnic table and watched some kids playing basketball.

"We'd better be ready to get back to the fire house," Mary said. "It looks like we're going to get some rain."

The clouds looked dark to Rainie, but they weren't very big.

"I'd think that'd get boring," Mary said, indicating Ryan's and Carl McDaniel's game of catch.

"Ryan will play for hours if he gets someone to play with him," explained Rainie.

"It's not going to be boring much longer," Mary said. "Here comes T.R." A kid with a dirty black cowboy hat walked toward the game. With the hat he was a little taller than Ryan.

"Who?" Rainie asked.

"T.R. Holton. Some call him Trouble, but mostly he's called Terror."

T.R. jumped in front of Ryan and barehanded the ball.

"Hey!" Carl yelled. "Come on T.R."

"Yeah, anyway, give that back!" Ryan yelled.

"Oh no, your brother shouldn't have said that," Mary exclaimed. "He's in for it now."

T.R. threw the ball down and then kicked Ryan's feet out from under him. Then he pounced on Ryan and shoved his face in the dirt and gravel. "What'd you say?" he demanded. "No skinny city kid tells me what to do!"

Mary ran toward the fight; Rainie followed.

Mary knocked T.R.'s hat off and grabbed his hair. She jerked backward so hard that T.R. slammed on his tailbone in the gravel. T.R. howled in pain.

"That's not the way we treat visitors, T.R.," declared Mary.

"Quit picking on me. I'll get you next," he yelled trying to stand.

Mary took a step backward and jerked him

down again. "I'm not afraid of you." Turning to Rainie, she said, "Go to the meeting and get my brother Yance. Just ask for Yance."

Rainie hated to leave with Ryan in such a state. She handed him his hat. His forehead was scraped and his right cheek had impressions in it, like he'd slept in the gravel. One tear streaked down the dirty cheek. It was the first time that Rainie had seen Ryan cry since Dad had left.

She started toward the fire house.

"Stop," T.R. yelled. "I give."

Mary let go of his hair. "Remember, we don't treat guests that way. Now get."

T.R. brushed his clothes off and retrieved his hat. He started toward the basketball game.

"I'm sorry about Terror." Carl handed Ryan his ball.

Rainie turned to Mary, "Thanks."

They started back to the fire house together.

"What's your brother like?" Rainie asked.

Mary smiled and said, "He's taller than my dad, but only half as mean."

They turned the corner and walked up the road. Raindrops splattered on the pavement. They ran to the fire house.

12

A New Brother

"We've got to hurry home," Uncle Matt said. "A canyon isn't the place to be if it's raining."

"Why?" asked Rainie.

"If it's raining up the canyon, then there's danger of flash floods. I think we're okay though, this storm is coming from behind us. But we need to make sure it doesn't get ahead of us."

"What happens if it does?" Rainie asked.

"We'll have to find a high place and wait for the flood to pass."

Rainie sighed. She'd wanted to see the petroglyph again. She prayed the rain would stop.

"It's strike two," Ryan pouted. He had his hat pulled low over the scrape on his forehead.

Rainie explained about T.R. and the fight.

"Well, it appears that Mary isn't anything like

her dad," Uncle Matt said. "But what's this about two strikes?"

"I had to be rescued again and this time it was a girl." Ryan buried his face in his hat.

Rainie thought Uncle Matt would say something, but he was silent. She noticed the rain had lost its driving sound.

"Since I've been here, everything's gone wrong." Ryan looked miserable. "It's like I'm waiting for the third strike."

"No one bats a thousand," offered Uncle Matt. Ryan turned to the window. "Everyone needs a coach, even the best hitters," Uncle Matt continued. "You've been trying to bat a thousand without a coach."

Ryan looked down as though he had something in his hands.

"Ryan, it's like this. If we took everyone in the world and lined them up on the coast of California and told them all to swim to Hawaii, who would make it?"

"No one," Ryan said.

"Everyone would need to be rescued. We are all just like those people drowning in the Pacific Ocean, only we all need to be rescued from our sin, from the trouble we get ourselves in, and from hell. Everyone needs Jesus as their Savior, because we all are sinners."

Rainie prayed for her uncle and for Ryan. The rain had slowed to a drizzle.

"God sent His Son Jesus to rescue us from our

sins and to give us eternal life. That's why Jesus died for us, to give us new life," Uncle Matt explained. "He wants to be our coach."

The rain had stopped. The sun peeked over the ridge and lit the black rock face above them.

"Look," Rainie said.

Uncle Matt stopped the pickup. They got out and looked up at the petroglyph. Its brown lines stuck out, its pyramid design clear in the bright beam that illuminated the rock wall above.

"I prayed for this," Rainie said. "Look how God answered."

"It's amazing," Uncle Matt said. "God certainly does wonderful things." Clouds blocked part of the sun and now only the rock face with the petroglyph shone.

Rainie remembered her uncle's words "like a road sign." The design looked like steps going up and steps going down. Maybe it meant go up, go down. She glanced up the walls of the canyon. About two hundred yards up the canyon, the wall on the right side was broken by a green slope. "I think this sign told the Indians to go up and over instead of traveling in the bottom," she said.

"Inspector Rainie rides again." Ryan smiled.

"Can we check that slope?" Rainie asked.

"Why don't you walk up the road and check?" Uncle Matt said. "Ryan and I will be there in a few minutes."

Rainie trotted up the road until she was across from the slope. A trail zigzagged up to the top. A sweet smell hung in the air, like the afterscent of rain, but mixed with a plant scent. It smelled sweet, like cinnamon.

She took off her shoes and waded across the stream. Horse tracks were barely visible in spite of the rain. Some were shallow pools of muddy water. Maybe they could catch the pot hunters now. She knew there had to be a road above.

Rainie put on her shoes and waited. The sun dipped behind the ridge. When Uncle Matt and Ryan drove up, she could tell by Ryan's red eyes that he'd been crying.

"Rainie, he's more than just your brother now. He's your new brother in the Lord," exclaimed Uncle Matt.

Rainie hugged Ryan for the first time she could remember.

13

Soap Circles Connect

Rainie rubbed the soap piece between her thumb and forefinger; she knew it had to be after midnight. The light should've appeared over an hour ago.

She'd explained everything at supper—how the pot hunters avoided passing the McDaniel place and how they parked above and then rode down into the canyon. Uncle Matt had helped her find the road on a forest service map. They figured it was only a half mile from the slope where the pot hunters entered the box. They probably brought their horses by horse trailer and parked above.

No one had noticed the soap circles but Aunt Amie. And she'd discovered them only because Rainie had mentioned the piece of soap. What surprised them was Rainie's explanation of the vanishing lights.

For an instant the first night the light had been bright; then it had gone out. Rainie believed the pot hunters worked under a make-shift black plastic tent. The first night either someone lit the lantern too early or the wind blew their tent over and put out the light. After that they made sure the lights were out at the ranch house before they started to work. The weird glow was the masked lantern light through the black plastic.

Now they were all waiting, even Cinch and Val; although Cinch was snoring on the couch.

"I think their being late can only mean one thing," Uncle Matt said.

"What?" Rainie asked.

"Whoever's doing this was at the meeting today."

"Did you see somebody with the diamond shape on their boot?" asked Ryan.

"I'm sorry Rainie, but you forgot to look at the bottom of my boots," Uncle Matt said.

Even in the dark room Rainie could tell by the teasing tone in his voice that Uncle Matt was smiling.

"Matthew," Aunt Amie scolded.

Rainie had never heard her aunt use her uncle's full name.

"Okay," he said in a chastened, but still teasing, sound. "If someone was at the meeting, it would take them time to get home, time to eat, time to load horses in a trailer, and travel time on that back road. Then you have to add to that the saddling and packing of horses, and then travel time from there up the box to the ruins."

"How fast can a horse travel?" Rainie asked.

"About three miles an hour on level ground," Uncle Matt said. "It's probably a three and a half mile trip for them and they have to come down that slope."

"So it'd be way over an hour," Rainie said.

"Maybe close to two," Uncle Matt said. "It might still be a while if it was someone from the meeting."

Rainie thought the light was never going to appear.

A half an hour later Rainie suddenly announced, "There it is!"

"How did you notice it?" Uncle Matt asked. The dim glow was like dying embers.

"If it hadn't been for that flare of light the first night, I wouldn't have been suspicious," explained Rainie.

"I'm glad you didn't listen to us," Ryan said. "We, I mean, I didn't believe you."

Rainie aligned herself with the table and then circled the light on the glass.

"Jesus said in John 10:10, 'The thief comes only to kill and steal and destroy, I came that they might have abundant life,'" Aunt Amie exclaimed. "I wonder if Rainie isn't right. Maybe there is more than just pot hunting going on up there."

"The light at the fort," Rainie said. "It still bothers me. What were they doing there?"

"Maybe they've been stealing with an intent to destroy," Aunt Amie offered. "If they destroyed the ruins, what would there be left for a national monument?"

"No crooks have a chance with you two on their tracks," Uncle Matt teased.

"Can we check the new circle in the morning?" Rainie begged.

"I was planning on it," Uncle Matt said.

"And the fort?" Ryan added.

"Are you trying to be a detective, too?" Uncle Matt said.

"What are we going to do after we check the ruins?" Rainie asked.

"You're not the only one who has secrets," Uncle Matt said. "I'll tell you my plan in the morning."

They heard snoring in the background. In the excitement, they'd forgotten to wake up Cinch. And Val had gone to sleep, too.

14

Dynamite

"What is your plan?" Rainie asked.

"I didn't bug you about your mystery," Uncle Matt teased. "Now you don't bug me about mine."

"But when?" Ryan asked.

"Maybe in a little while," answered Uncle Matt.

They'd had breakfast and skipped their riding lesson. Now they were balancing on rocks again crossing the creek. The third soap circle indicated the opposite side of the pueblo ruin. Rainie thought Aunt Amie was right; the thief had come to steal and destroy.

Ryan crossed first and ran up the toe of the bench. "More diamond tracks," he yelled back, "and three more rooms have been dug into."

Uncle Matt and Rainie inspected the area, but couldn't find any more clues. Ryan lost interest and began to chase lizards.

"I can't catch a single lizard," Ryan complained. "There're too many rocks for them to hide under and they're too fast for me."

Rainie reflected on Ryan's decision to accept Christ as his Savior. She could already see changes in him, like admitting that the lizards were too fast for him. Two days ago he would never have admitted that he was second to anyone or anything.

Ryan returned, puffing, from his lizard chase. "What part of the fort are we going to look at?"

"The loose soil across from the big hole," Rainie said, "where we first discovered the diamond tracks."

"If there is any digging to be done," Uncle Matt cautioned, "I'll do it. That's part of the plan."

Rainie and Ryan ran ahead.

"Wait at the doorway," Uncle Matt yelled.

Rainie and Ryan paused.

"Let me catch my breath," Uncle Matt panted. "My legs and lungs aren't as young as yours. Next time we'll use the horses."

Uncle Matt entered the ruin first. "The tracks have been washed out by the rain."

"They were almost in the corner," Rainie directed.

"Umm, listen, if I tell you to run," Uncle Matt said, "I want instant obedience. I have an idea this could turn out to be dangerous." He knelt and started digging gently.

Rainie and Ryan bent over Uncle Matt while he worked. Rainie had guessed right.

Only six inches down, Uncle Matt found the destroyer—three sticks of dynamite with a yellow cap attached. "This is what I was afraid I'd find."

"Wow, dynamite! This is just like in the movies," exclaimed Ryan.

"Now, I've got to pull this cap from the primer," Uncle Matt said. "Get down the bench to the creek. I'm going to count to a hundred and then I'm going to pull. You've got to be far away in case anything goes wrong."

Rainie and Ryan obeyed. Rainie counted and prayed for her uncle's safety as she walked away. "One hundred and twenty-five," she said aloud, "I think everything's okay."

They heard the crunching sound of steps coming toward them. Uncle Matt appeared with the cap in his hand. "I'm glad that's done. Let's get back to the ranch so I can rest my nerves."

At lunch Uncle Matt revealed his plan. "Tonight we're going to try and help the sheriff catch the vandals. So we'd better get good naps this afternoon."

"Do you think they planted dynamite all around the ruins?" Ryan asked.

"I'm sure they did," Uncle Matt said. "Whoever did this isn't playing games."

"You said there was a bigger pueblo ruin across from the fort on this side of the canyon," Rainie said.

Uncle Matt turned and pointed out the window.

"See that taller bench just across the arroyo past our fenceline." Then he paused as though in thought. "It's higher and harder for us to see."

"Maybe we should check it," Ryan suggested.

"Val, you'd better check it this afternoon," Uncle Matt said.

"But . . ." Ryan started to complain.

"If you don't get a nap, you'll be too tired to go tonight."

"Ahem," Aunt Amie cleared her voice. "I think the most important thing is prayer. We'd better pray for God's protection for all of you."

They held hands and prayed.

15

Stake-out

The sun set in a splash of orange and red flames just as Rainie, Ryan, Cinch and Uncle Matt started down the box. The creek water sloshed against the pickup.

"It feels like we're in a boat," Rainie said as they drove through the water.

"Red sky in morning, sailor take warning," Uncle Matt said in response to the brilliant sunset.

"What does that mean?" Ryan asked.

"If there's a red sky in the morning, there will be a storm later in the day."

"What about red in the evening?" Rainie asked.

"The weather will be fair," said Uncle Matt.

"The sky sure must have been red yesterday morning," Ryan said, "because I sure went through a storm."

"But because of the storm," Rainie said, "you

found the Lord."

Ryan smiled.

"So you're telling us everything's going to work out okay tonight," Rainie said. She enjoyed the mysterious mood her uncle was in and she thought Ryan had been caught up in it too.

"We prayed," Uncle Matt said, "and the plan's in place. Now, we just have to wait for the vandals."

"If they show up," Cinch said from his crunched position next to the pickup door.

"They'll show up," Rainie said. "They came at least one night before we noticed them."

"Before *you* noticed them," Uncle Matt corrected.

"I wonder if they're going to destroy more of the ruin Val searched today?" Rainie asked.

"They might even blow everything up," Ryan said.

"What if they do?" Rainie asked.

"We've done everything we could do," Uncle Matt said. "The rest is in the Lord's hands."

By the time they reached the slope where the vandals had been coming down, it was almost pitch black. And the moon was barely a sliver in the sky.

"We'll drive down and hide the pickup around the bend of the canyon just past the petroglyph," Uncle Matt explained. "Then we'll hide in the willows not far from the slope. After they pass, we'll wait another twenty minutes. Then Cinch will go down to McDaniels to call the sheriff and we'll go up to find their truck and trailer."

"How are we going to catch them?" Ryan asked.

"We're not going to catch them. That's the sheriff's job. We're just going to make sure they get caught."

"But how?" insisted Ryan.

He winked at Rainie and then said, "That's a surprise."

After they parked the truck, Uncle Matt said, "But before we do anything else, we've got to put this on." He sprayed insect repellent on his hands and then wiped it on his face and the back of his neck. Then he put a small pack on his back.

As they walked back up the road to their hiding place, they took turns putting on the repellent.

"They may not hear us," Cinch said, "but they'll sure smell us."

"They won't hear us if you stay awake," Rainie teased.

"You pinch him if he nods off, Ryan," Uncle Matt said.

"No, you won't," Cinch said, "I'm staying awake."

As they neared the hiding place, Uncle Matt said, "We're going to sit still until after they've passed. Don't anyone even think about making a sound."

They positioned themselves in a clump of willows about fifty yards from the slope.

Rainie couldn't believe how many sounds broke the night. Small animals rustled through the undergrowth. She caught herself unconsciously roll-

ing her bracelet when she thought about things
that slithered. She prayed.

The clink of horseshoes against stone echoed
from above; then the silhouette of three riders and
a pack horse appeared in the dim moonlight. One
rider was considerably shorter than the others.

"It's T.R.," Ryan whispered.

Rainie put her finger to his lips. Maybe Ryan was
right. The shorter rider looked T.R.'s size and one
of the others could be T.R.'s dad, Mr. Holton. But
who was the third? Maybe it was another rancher
who feared his ranch was going to be taken by the
government.

After the horses splashed by, it seemed to Rainie
like they waited forever. Finally, Uncle Matt took
out a canteen and they all got a drink. Then he
passed each a flashlight and Cinch left.

They took off their shoes and crossed the creek.

"Do you think that was T.R. and Mr. Holton?"
Rayn asked as he stepped out of the creek.

"I'm not sure," Uncle Matt said. "It was too dark
to tell." He held his flashlight so Rainie and Ryan
could put on their shoes.

"I wonder who the third rider was?" Rainie
asked.

"Probably one of T.R.'s mean friends," Ryan
said.

"Here, hold the light," Uncle Matt said.

Rainie grabbed the light and held it as Uncle
Matt balanced on one foot and pulled on his boot.

"Make sure you stay close," Uncle Matt said

after he finished pulling on his second boot. "If you get tired, say so. We'll stop and rest."

The trail zigzagged back and forth across the slope. All three were puffing when they reached the top.

"What if they left someone with the trailer?" Rainie whispered.

"I hadn't thought about that," said Uncle Matt. "We'll have to travel without the lights."

Uncle Matt led, but much slower than before.

"Ouch," Ryan almost yelled.

Uncle Matt helped Ryan get unhooked from a mesquite branch and whispered, "Wait here."

Ryan and Rainie waited about five minutes and then they saw Uncle Matt's light coming back.

"There's no one here. You can use your lights."

When they reached the pickup and trailer, Uncle Matt handed them two small sticks.

"Is this the surprise?" Ryan asked.

The vandals had turned the truck and trailer around so they were ready to get away. Uncle Matt led them to the pickup's left side.

"Now what?" Ryan asked.

"Let the air out of the tires and then we'll get back down the trail," said Uncle Matt.

Ryan finished first and then moved to the trailer tire and started unscrewing the valve cap.

"Two's enough," said Uncle Matt.

"Wait," Rainie whispered as they moved toward the trail. "Listen."

The distant clink of horseshoes rang out.

"Someone's coming," Rainie whispered.

"What if they have guns?" Ryan asked.

Uncle Matt quickly searched the pickup bed with his flashlight and then grabbed a lug wrench.

"What will that do against guns!" Ryan exclaimed.

"Quiet," Rainie whispered.

"I'm sorry kids," Uncle Matt said softly as he held up the lug wrench as though ready to strike. "I didn't expect this to turn out this way. Pray hard."

The creaking sound of a saddle grew closer.

They rushed behind the trailer and then to its tongue. The rider tied the horse to the back of the trailer. They ducked behind the trailer as the rider walked to the trailer's right side.

"Who's there?" the rider asked.

16

Waters Calm

Uncle Matt shone his light on Mary Yancey.

"Don't hit me," Mary's frightened voice echoed in the darkness.

Uncle Matt put his arm down and set the lug wrench in the pickup bed. "I'm sorry," he sid, "I didn't mean to scare you."

"What are you doing?" Ryan yelled. "She might have a gun!"

"Come on," Uncle Matt said and put his hand on Ryan's shoulder. "We'll go meet the sheriff."

"What if she tries to get away?" Ryan asked.

"She's not going to run away," Uncle Matt said. "Are you?"

Mary shook her head and looked down at her feet.

When Uncle Matt and Ryan left, Rainie asked,

"Why, Mary?"

"Dad promised me a pickup if I helped."

"You must have had more reason than that."

"Fear, I guess." Mary sat on the trailer wheel-well and Rainie stood next to her. "Dad kept saying we were going to lose our land. He said if we destroyed the ruins, the government wouldn't need our land because there wouldn't be anything left to make into a park or monument."

Rainie saw headlights off in the distance and the figures of her brother and uncle in the lights. They'd met the sheriff. Other figures appeared in the lights and then the headlights went out.

"Why'd you come back?" asked Rainie.

"Dad sent me back," Mary said. "But it was strange. Not a mile down the canyon he stopped and for some reason checked the detonator. He'd put new batteries in it when we left home, but the batteries wouldn't work."

"You were going to blow up the ruins tonight?"

"If the batteries had worked," Mary said. "He sent me back to get more, but he knew there weren't any. He told me to get some sleep if I didn't find any."

"Then what were they going to do?"

"Dig some more pots. Yance said Dad was getting greedy. We should've stopped before this, but Dad said he wanted as many pots as possible before he blew up the ruins."

"Why was he going to blow up the ruins tonight?" asked Rainie.

"Only because Yance and I were afraid of getting caught," Mary answered.

Rainie turned when she heard the approach of the men on the road. Several flashlight beams bounced on the road as the men walked up to the trailer.

"Rainie, one of the deputies is going to give us a lift back to the McDaniels," Uncle Matt said. Three policemen stood next to him and Ryan.

"Mary, I want you to have this," Rainie said as she held out her bracelet. "When you touch it I want you to remember that Jesus loves you and that I'm praying for you."

Rainie stood at the picture window now, and thought about last night. The window washing liquid and rag were on the sill. But she didn't want to wash the window yet.

After the deputy had dropped them off at the McDaniels, they'd had a good laugh; Cinch was asleep across the seat snoring again. Then they'd driven the long way home, so as not to meet the Yanceys in the box.

Ryan had said the waters were calm now, and for Ryan they were. It was still hard to believe that Ryan had accepted Jesus as his Savior. But the changes in Ryan already spoke of God's working in his life. The waters were calm for Ryan and Rainie, but what about the ranchers? Until the ranchers' fear of their lands being taken was eliminated, the waters could be easily stirred.

Rainie looked out at the cattle grazing below the fort ruins. She hadn't really noticed them before; she'd been concentrating on solving the mystery of the vanishing lights.

Then the idea struck her. Ranchers fenced in cattle; why couldn't they fence out people?

"Aunt Amie!" she yelled as she rushed into the office.

"Good heavens girl, what's wrong?"

"I've got an idea," Rainie said. "What if the ranchers got together and built a security fence around the ruins? That would keep the people out and maybe the local museums could give tours to people who wanted to see the ruins."

"That's a great idea." Aunt Amie's voice sounded as excited as Rainie's. "Then the ruins could still be preserved and the land wouldn't have to become a monument."

Rainie wanted to tell Uncle Matt, but she knew the men and Ryan were out fixing fences. Uncle Matt had teased that her mysteries had put them behind in their ranch work.

Her mind was at ease about the ranchers. She could wash the window now. But as she looked at the gash they called Monticello Box, she remembered the petroglyph. It had helped solve the mystery, but why had the Indians put it there? What was up and over the hill?

Glossary

adobe—a brick or building material of sun-dried earth and straw; a heavy clay used in making adobe bricks; a structure made of adobe bricks.

arroyo—a deep, dry gully in a dry area that usually only fills with water after a recent rain.

bench—a flat area of land that at an earlier time was the shore of a sea or lake or the floodplain of a river.

box—a canyon with an opening at only one end which makes it useful as a large "corral" for rounding up livestock.

cobble pueblo—the communal dwelling of an Indian village of Arizona and New Mexico.

corral—a pen or enclosure for capturing livestock.

grulla—a horse with a smoky, grayish-blue or mouse-colored coat with dark points, a stripe on its back and often zebra-like markings on the legs, shoulders, and ears.

heeler—a type of dog used for herding livestock.

mesquite—a spiny deep-rooted tree or shrub that forms in extensive thickets, bears pods rich in sugar, and is important as livestock feed. Commonly found in the southwestern United States and Mexico.

petroglyph—a carving or inscription on a rock.

timberline—the highest elevation that trees can grow on mountains.

Now that you've finished the book, perhaps we can help you solve another mystery . . .

You may be wondering what Rainie and Ryan meant when they talked about being "saved." The answer to this mystery can be found in God's Word, the Bible:

The Bible says, "I [Jesus] have come that they may have life, and have it to the full" (John 10:10). Jesus said He came to give us life—not just a happy life now, but a life that will last forever in heaven. If you are not living life "to the full" as Jesus wants you to, there is a reason why:

The Bible says, "For all have sinned and fall short of the glory of God" (Romans 3:23). Sin is anything you do that you know is wrong, or anything you don't do that you know you should. Uncle Matt told Rainie that, just as stirring up the water in a pool makes it cloudy, sin stirs things up so we can't see things clearly—and we "fall short" of the life God wants us to have.

The Bible says, "For the wages of sin is death" (Romans 6:23). Not only does sin make us "fall short" of the full life God wants for us now, it also makes us die—we lose our chance to live forever in heaven. If that is true, we're in big trouble, aren't we? We need someone to rescue us—someone to "save" us.

And that is just what happened!

The Bible says, "You see, at just the right time, when we were still powerless, Christ died for the ungodly" (Romans 5:6). Jesus Christ, the Son of God, came to earth as a man and died in our place. He took the punishment we deserved—He came to rescue us!

That's what the word *Savior* means—Jesus Christ *saved* us from death.

The Bible says, "He [Jesus] is the atoning sacrifice for our sins" (1 John 2:2). The word *atoning* means to pay for. When Jesus died on the cross, He paid for all the sins we ever did and ever will do. Isn't that wonderful? The Apostle Paul calls it a gift—the best gift we could ever get.

How do we receive this gift?

The Bible says, "Believe in the Lord Jesus, and you will be saved" (Acts 16:31). We have to believe that Jesus really did what the Bible says He did—died for our sins. But He did more than that—He also rose from the dead to prove that He has the power to give us eternal life.

The Bible says, "If you confess with your mouth, 'Jesus is Lord,' and believe in your heart that God raised him from the dead, you will be saved" (Romans 10:9). Part of believing in Jesus is making Him our Lord (our boss, our leader) and letting Him have control of our life.

Will you do that today? If so, why not pray the following prayer, then write your name and the date on the space below as a record of what you have done?

Dear Lord Jesus, I believe that You died on the cross for my sins. I ask You now to forgive me of my sins. I confess that You are Lord and that God has raised You from the dead. I take You now as my Savior and Lord.

*Name*_____

Date _____

If you have truly done that, and have turned from your sins, congratulations! You are now a Christian—a member of God's family! This is an important step you've taken, and you should tell someone about it—your parents, your pastor, your friends.

Another important step to take is to get to know your new Friend, Jesus. One of the best ways to get to know Him and to learn what He expects of you is to read the Bible. Do you remember how Rainie, after studying the petroglyph, discovered that it was like a road sign for the ancient Indians? The Bible is also like a road sign—it tells you the way to go. And like the petroglyph, you need to study it carefully to see what the Lord is telling you.

Congratulations again—and welcome to the family of God!